VOICES

Voices

by

Kit Power

Black Shuck Books
www.BlackShuckBooks.co.uk

Versions of the following stories first appeared as follows:
'Baptism' in *Widowmakers* (2014)
'Like a Charm' in *KZine* (Issue 14, January 2016)
'Enemies' and 'The Hand' in *A Warning About Your Future Enslavement That You Will Dismiss As A Collection Of Short Fiction And Essays By Kit Power* (2017)

Cover design & internal layout © WHITEspace 2019
www.white-space.uk

First published in the UK by Black Shuck Books, 2020

978-1-913038-46-5

This book is dedicated with love, affection and respect to the main man, Stephen King.

'On Writing' gave me permission to find my voice. Whatever modest success I enjoy is thanks to that permission. I will continue to write about what scares me.

Baptism

So, you would have my confession? Very well, I give it freely. Still, I beg you, do not interrupt with your confounding questions, though I know you will have many. Save them until the end. That which I must tell, I would tell once through, lest I lose my nerve. Attend, then, and transcribe faithfully.

It was a normal Wednesday evening. I had completed work in my study at the usual hour, and taken my supper with Isabelle. She was her usual delightful self – questioning, laughing, the spirit of gaiety alive in her shining eyes and rosy cheeks...

...Forgive me.

The tub had been prepared as normal, the large basin placed by the roaring fire, the water pleasantly warm but not hot. After our meal,

Isabelle and I retired to the living room. The maid was dismissed, and Isabelle allowed me to disrobe her, giggling as I tickled her naked arms, squealing with delight when my whiskers brushed her belly.

She loved to laugh.

I lifted her into the tub, and bathed her, talking to her as I did so about my day. I let her splash a little, watched her spread out and pretend to swim, my arms leaning on the edge of the tub, waiting to reach in and grasp her if she were to slip.

I washed her hair with soap, then blew some bubbles between my thumb and forefinger, her high voice encouraging me to increase their size, her laughter flowing like some sweet warming nectar.

I had turned to the fire, reaching for a jug of clean water to rinse her hair, when the change occurred. When I turned away, she had been excitedly describing the bubbles, remarking on their different sizes. This had continued as I turned, but as my hand neared the handle of the jug, her voice transformed. Mid word, it dropped, first low, then high, then low, alternating on each syllable. At the same time, the words vanished, replaced by a nonsensical babble.

"Da-BOO-Rah-JAK-ka-SAL-Ood."

Each lower register seemed deeper than the last, each high note louder and more shrill. I cannot fully put into words the terror that struck me in this moment, how horrified I was by that apparently senseless noise. Something in the alternating register, the apparently random sounds, struck dread into me, as though I were hearing some awful incantation.

As if in sympathy with my panic, the large log in the centre of the fire split with a loud crack. Smoking embers flew into the deep rug and began to smoulder.

"Joh-RAY-Lin-GAR-Den-DOO-Sal-REF-Moo..."

"Isabelle! Stop!"

I was still looking to the fire, attention caught by the tendrils of smoke rising from the rug, and my panic gave my voice a timbre and gruffness that would ordinarily command obedience, possibly even tears. I had a moment to curse my own harshness, to wonder at why I should be so gripped with emotion as to address her with such temper.

Then the babble rose again.

As I close my eyes, I hear it still, every dread syllable. But I dare not repeat it. Suffice it to say, her voice deepened further, hitting notes that were surely not possible, and the high notes became screeches that grated my senses raw. The flames in the fire began to surge, burning hotter, the coals glowing fiercely. The smoke from the rug was becoming thicker, darker, and I saw flame begin to flicker.

In a spasm of movement, I grabbed one of the jugs and poured it out over the smouldering rug. I heard the angry hiss of water becoming steam, but observed that the flames had been extinguished.

At the same time I felt the heat from the fire increase again, becoming more intense, seeming to be drawn to ferocity by the inhuman noises my darling daughter was producing, though in truth by then I scarcely recognised her voice. My eyes returned to the flames, squinting against the heat, and there I saw...

There I saw the fire, receding and growing, falling back and away. The fireplace around it grew faint and faded, then too the ground on which it sat sunk, as though melting in the heat, DON'T LOOK AT ME LIKE THAT!

DON'T!

...

Forgive me. Forgive me. It... No, no, you weren't there. Let me tell it, quickly.

The ground fell away, before my unbelieving eyes, until I was kneeling upon a pillar of rock, surrounded on all sides by darkness, and a sheer drop. Far beneath me, as far as my eyes could see, fire spread in all directions, flickering and rolling. The babble had become a chant, the deep parts guttural as a mad dog, the high notes shrieking like a bird of prey, the devilish syllables seeming to warp my mind as surely as they warped the world around us. Boiling waves of heat rose from the pit, singeing my eyebrows, burning the very air in my throat.

My head turned back to the tub, seemingly of its own volition, and I beheld her.

Her skin had turned red, and her eyes glowed a sickly yellow, as though lit from inside by a flame burning some noxious substance. Her smile had become a leer of perfect depravity, pointed teeth pushing out at crazed angles from bloody gums, her lips splitting in places as the grin pushed her mouth unnaturally wide, as though whatever was passing through her by invocation was tearing her apart as it transformed her. I beheld her, but knew her not, and when her eyes met mine, I saw only damnation: Mine, hers, perhaps the world's.

I acted on pure instinct. Though her size had increased somewhat, she was still an infant in basic form, so it was a simple matter to grab her legs and pull. Her red skin was almost painfully warm to the touch, but my grip held firm, and her head slipped beneath the surface of the water with ease.

I shifted my body, moving my hands to hold her shoulders, fearing that mouth, those teeth. I saw understanding dawn across that hideous visage, and then a ferocious rage that seemed almost to stab out at me; certainly I felt my heart lurch in my chest, but the fear that had galvanised me to action held me in its grip, and I maintained the downward pressure as the monster began to thrash.

How it struggled! The water churned and roiled as I wrestled with the inhuman figure. It seemed to last an age, long enough for me to wonder if perhaps this dread creature could somehow breathe underwater, but gradually the struggles began to lessen, and I felt the awesome heat begin to dissipate, to withdraw. I perceived at the edge of my vision that the world was assuming its rightful shape once more, even as the creature in my hand began to shrink, to fade from that hellish, bloody hue, to the soft pastel pink of my beloved Isabelle.

I beheld her there, once again perfect. My darling daughter. She lay at the bottom of the tub, beyond all pain, all misery, all love. At peace.

I sobbed for a while, before ringing for the maid. She in turn called for the constabulary, and there you found me.

This is my story. I will not tell it again. Do as you must, as your conscience and laws dictate. I pray only that the end be swift, and that afterwards I see her restored. That I might hear that beautiful laugh once more.

I desire nothing else.

I'm not much of a writer. I know you're gonna think I'm crazy. I'm OK with that. This is the truth. Believe what you want, I'm past caring. I just want to lay it all out, once and for all.

Started at a gun show. My rookie year, '96. I was looking for a piece for Janie. Things were getting serious. I wanted something she could carry for protection. She was an army brat. Didn't take much persuading.

I was browsing a trinket stall. Looking for something that would wind up my dipshit liberal brother. Bumper sticker, T-Shirt, 'cold dead hands', something like that. I remember I was deep in it, so when the guy said, "Can I help you, officer?" it made me jump.

I turned around. Took him in. He was 5' 7", short spiked red hair, freckles, clean shaven, 'cold dead hands' T ('there it is', I thought), combat pants. Dog tags. Novelty ones that read 'Yeah, I was in the shit'. Slim build. Classic chickenhawk/rooster type. He spread his hands at hip height, but he was smiling, pleased with himself.

"Hey, sorry, no offence meant. But you are a cop, right?"

I considered not answering, or lying. But what the fuck. Might as well get used to it. "No. But I'm gonna be. I graduate next week."

"Hey, congratulations, officer!" His handshake was solid, dry, brief. "Thank you for your service."

"Sure."

Wasn't the first time I'd heard it and it sure wouldn't be the last. There was a period after nine eleven when it was all anyone could say, seemed like. But it was new enough then to still feel awkward.

"Hey, we've got a twenty percent discount for cops and soldiers. Ambulance workers too, but we don't get as many of those." Shrug. "What you in the market for?"

"Just browsing." Polite. Keeping my distance.

I remember how he looked at me then.

Staring. Like he was trying to make his mind up about something. I didn't like it.

"How about a good luck charm? I know, I know..." – reading my face – "...sounds hokey. Hell, it is hokey, but still. Who couldn't use a little luck now and again? Especially in this town. Am I right?" He flashed a big grin. So sincere and goofy I couldn't help but smile back, against my will.

"Sure."

"Sure! Great! Okay, here we go then..." There was a drawer underneath the table. As he pulled it out, I saw rows and rows of small plastic boxes piled deep. Hundreds, looked like. He ran his finger across them. Glancing up at my face then back down. Frowning. Concentrating.

It felt odd, uncomfortable, but I figured he was driving at something and I was curious. His eyes flicked up again, three times, four, then "Okay, try this one!"

He held the box up to me. Inviting me to take it. I took it up to eye level. There was a fine silver chain, looped through a small glass or plastic cylinder. Inside that, a single bullet. Looked like a big one, a .44 or .45. Looking close, I could see scratches across the surface of the slug.

"Here."

He handed me a jeweller's magnifying glass. Smiling again, but a little nervous. Like a con-man feeling his mark swaying in the breeze. I didn't like it, but I took it anyway and looked. Somehow I knew what I was going to see. Sure enough, engraved across the surface of the slug was the word 'John'.

The feeling of knowing, then seeing, made me start. He laughed, clapping his hands together once. Sharp and loud. "Yes! I guessed right, didn't I?"

Really pleased with himself. I saw no sense in denying it.

"Neat trick. How did you do it?"

He shrugged again, all aw shucks.

"Dunno, honestly. I get it wrong as often as right. But, shit, I dunno, you look like a John." He shrugged again. Apologetic.

"Well, what do you think? A bullet, with your name on? Better you have it than someone else, right?"

He smiled again. Again I felt my own face respond. He seemed harmless, after all.

"How much?"

"Tell you what, just pull a bill out your wallet blind, and I'll take it."

I thought about it. The biggest bill I had was a $20, and... "Sure? I know I've got some singles in there."

"What can I say? I feel like gambling. Must be in the air. Come on, take it as an apology for spooking you earlier. My bad."

Sincere, suddenly.

I pulled out a bill blind and handed it over, not looking. He laughed. "Lincoln, huh?" He shook his head, still grinning. "That'll teach me! Shit, could have been worse. Here you go, sir."

He handed me over the box.

"Don't go losing it, now!" he said. Salesman smile sliding back into place.

~

I graduated as advertised. Married Janie in the fall. Got started in LVPD. Partnered up. Foot patrol. Car patrol. Drunks and whores and pimps and pushers. Vegas was going for the 'family destination' dollar again. We had plenty to keep us busy, trying to keep all that shit off the strip where it liked to be, down back in the ghettos where it belonged. Lots of busts. The odd broken head. Beers with the boys of an evening. The odd double date with the other married guys. Janie on the pill, not in any hurry to start in on the kids thing.

Good times.

The bullet just sat in my wallet. Forgotten.

Most cops are superstitious, at least a little. Something about having your ass on the line every day. I saw a few St. Christophers, St. Michaels. Stuff like that. One guy had a poker chip from The Stardust. He claimed it had been in Frank Rosenthal's pocket the day he survived that car bombing. "This thing was in his pocket when his car exploded around him! And he walked away! You believe that shit?"

"Sure," I said.

Not everyone had a good luck charm, but most did.

Anyway.

Andy was my partner. A good kid. Pretty much a straight arrow. I knew that some of the others would sometimes catch a free blowjob from a whore. A bribe for not busting them. Later, when things started going bad, I took a few myself. But not Andy. I can't say that *no-one* deserves what happened to him – I've seen too much evil shit to think that – but he sure didn't.

It was late fall. The overnight shift. Car patrol on the strip. Call comes in.

Officer down.

It's close, ninety seconds out. We hit the blues. Andy floors it. I call it in.

I don't know the guy who's been shot. We're a big force, I've only been on the job eighteen months. Control says he's been responding to a call. Routine DMV. He's hit the red button. No voice contact since. No other info except the last known. I feel sick. Scared. Angry. Stomach like lead. My hands are steady enough as I unclip the holster of my sidearm. The street is lined with small, single story houses. Old cars out front. Battered plastic kids' toys out on the lawns.

Shitty neighbourhood.

The officer is lying in the middle of the street. On his back. Andy slams on the breaks. Tires screaming. ABS making the car shudder. I have time to see the blood pool under his body. Uniform gleaming with it. It looks bad.

We slide to a halt about ten feet away. One look. No words. We draw and get out of the car as one. Covering the houses that line the street. We walk sideways, backs to each other. Moving towards the cop. Looking for signs of movement.

"Anything?" Glad to hear my voice sounding calm. My heart beating about one twenty.

"Nope. Wait..."

I start to turn my head in his direction. That's when it happens. Explosion of sound from my side of the street. The flat crack of rifle fire. Semi-automatic.

My mind freezes. The training takes over. I hit the deck. My peripheral vision picks out Andy doing the same. I bring my gun up. My head turns back to my side of the street.

Time is running slooooow. I can hear each repeat of the rifle. Feel the breeze as a slug passes by my left cheek.

Some nights I wake up feeling that. Sweaty and scared.

Anyway.

I think that I need to get to cover. That we are sitting ducks. Then I see the muzzle flash from the ground floor window opposite. Instinct takes over.

I fired all fourteen rounds into the side of the house. Ballistics confirmed after that I'd hit the perp in six places, including the fatal headshot. At the time, all I knew was that the asshole had stopped shooting. I turned back to the other officer. Saw with no real surprise that he wasn't moving or breathing.

Andy was. He was also drooling blood and looked in a bad way. I dragged him into cover behind our car. Better safe than sorry. Waited for the cavalry.

The CSI boys were pretty surprised afterwards that the shooter had managed to miss me and hit Andy. They took a good look at the angle of the shooter. His field of vision relative to the two of us. Pretty easy to recreate, with the blood pools in the street, my spent casings, what have you. There was a fair bit of head-scratching all round.

"You musta hit the deck quicker, that's all." It was bullshit. I went along with it. No sense doing otherwise. I thought I just got lucky.

Andy, not so much. He arrested twice, once in the ambulance, once at the hospital. He went under for ten minutes the second time. He didn't come all the way back. Oxygen deprivation. Permanent brain damage. He ended up somewhere near functional, but lost all his speech memory. Had to learn to talk again from scratch. Lost some higher function too. Shitty business.

I'd always been a drinker. Most cops are. I started drinking for real not long after that. To start with, it was just to help me sleep. I kept waking up screaming. Feeling the breeze of a bullet passing my cheek. Again and again. Janie soon had me sleeping on the sofa most of the time. I was waking her up and freaking her out. Of course, that just made me drink more.

I managed to hide it from work. The drinking, the dreams, all of it. PTSD does not look good on a cop's resume, however PC the department was pretending to be. I went to the mandatory counselling, all that crap. I kept my shit together and to myself. Scored a clean bill of health.

TV makes you think that a cop's life is nothing but crazed villains and shoot outs. That's bullshit. It's mainly boring. Hard, mindless work, with occasional flashes of excitement. It was another five years before someone took a shot at me.

My next partner was Fred. Fred was a real piece of shit. Lazy. Dumb. Fucking gross personal habits. He'd belch loudly every time he ate, laugh like it was funny. He could pick his nose for hours, seemed like. Rooting around in there like he was digging for gold. He wasn't a trophy hunter. He ate what he caught.

He also had an appetite like a fucking hog. And the smallest bladder of any man I've ever known. Which meant that we'd end up stopping once an hour at the nearest food joint, so he could go for a piss and buy more junk on the way out to fill his face with. Goddamn car stank of stale food all the time. Made me want to puke.

That's how come we were outside the Double D downtown that afternoon. Him and his small bladder and his fat gut.

It happens fast. One second, we're standing next to the car in the lot, arguing about the relative merits of custard versus jelly. The next his face just fucking explodes. Rips apart, shredded. Splashing my own face with blood. A swarm of angry bees buzzes past my face. The boom of the shotgun blast echoes off the building behind me.

We stand there for a second, frozen. I see Fred try and swallow. The pellets have shredded his face so badly that I can see his tongue working against his teeth through the ragged hole in his cheek.

Then we both drop. Me into cover behind a

car. Him into a bleeding heap. I hit the panic button. Officer down. Draw my gun, but the black SUV has already pulled away.

In the movies the cop would shoot through the traffic. Somehow manage to only hit the bad guy's car. I just got the plates and called it in.

Turned out to be stolen. Local bangers had just brought in a new initiation test for the young bloods. Tag a cop, earn your colours. That gang didn't last the year, but the attack on me and my partner turned out to be the first skirmish of a bloody and nervy summer.

Not for Fred though. For him, the war was definitely over. No brain damage, but he lost an eye. All the plastic in the world, not to mention four months in hospital, couldn't put his face back together. He lost some speech too. Nerve damage to his jaw. Talked like he had a mouth full of cotton balls.

He took a medical discharge and pension. Six months after, on the first anniversary of the shooting, he finished the job with his own .45.

What happened before, to Andy, had messed me up. It was a walk in the park next to Fred. Not because of him – piece of shit. No. Just because…

I'd seen the gun fire out of the corner of my

eye. Seen the fire spitting out of the barrel. The eyes of a dragon coming to life. I'd known for sure that I was dead. My partner's face disintegrated and what seemed like a thousand pellets buzzed past my face, close enough to feel. To hear. Parting in front of my nose like Moses and the red sea.

The drinking got heavier. My marriage collapsed. She walked one evening while I was on shift. Left a Dear John. Sweet, really. Still caring. We had barely spoken in months. I could hardly remember her face, seemed like. Except, no. That's not right. I can picture her now, if I close my eyes. It's more like the face of a stranger though. Not connected to anything.

Anyhow. By then there was only the bottle and the job. And the job was starting to turn to shit.

Cop humour is legendarily black. What you may not realise is that it can also be very cruel. With two partners down in six years there were bound to be jokes. It started with a printed note taped to my locker: "To lose one partner is tragic. To lose two starts to look like carelessness."

I left it on there, to show I could take the joke. It ate at me. The other cops started to pull away too. Distance themselves. Offers to go out after a shift for beers or a meal seemed strained, insincere. They stopped asking long before the excuses turned stale. That was okay. By then I preferred drinking alone. Sometimes, when I was lying on my couch, trying to get drunk enough to sleep, I'd take the bullet out of my wallet and hold it up to the light. Look at it. Usually I'd pass out, eventually. Every time I woke up my fist would be closed around it. Holding it close.

Got through a lot of partners. The usual way. No-one wanted to work with me for long. A combination of my rep and my increasing distance. It was fine by me. I had no ambition beyond serving my twenty and getting my pension. I had a vague idea that if I could somehow do that, I could maybe get clean. Try and get a little bit of my life back. Drunk logic.

A DV call in '09 put paid to that. Jackson and me were the first responders. Neighbours report yelling. Breaking glass. Kids crying. In the two minutes it takes us to make the address dispatch give us an ex-husband and restraining order linked to the residence. A sheet long enough for us to realise whatever is going on tonight has probably been coming for a while.

None of this is new to me by this time, but my gut is tighter than normal. Because, kids.

"Okay, I say we've got P.C. so we go in heavy. You take the back, try and get the woman, kids out, if you can. I'll take the front, try and nail the suspect. Questions?"

"None." Jackson already has his piece drawn. Ready for a quick exit.

"Good. Kids're more likely to be at the rear, but stay sharp. If the perp is armed, he gets one warning – after that, he fails to comply in any fucking way, put him down. Do not try to be a hero. Got it?"

I flick my eyes from the road to Jackson's face for a second. He meets my gaze level. Nods quickly. He's got kids. I know he won't fuck about.

"Okay, let's do it."

I pull the car up outside the house, across the street. Kill the engine. The lights are on. There's yelling. Screaming. Crying.

"I'm giving you sixty, then I'm taking the door."

Jackson doesn't reply. Dives out the door and runs across the street. Low. Heading for the side alley.

I wait in the car for a slow thirty. Get out and walk across the street, up to the front door. Gun drawn and pointing at the ground. Heart beating slow but heavy.

I can hear kids crying. A woman screaming. My gut turns cold as I reach the door. The screen door is unlocked. Opens quietly. The door itself looks cheap. Like the house, the neighbourhood. Good. I draw a last breath, deep. Brace. Gun up now.

My kick splinters the thin wood around the lock. The door flies inward, banging off the interior wall, swinging back.

"Police!"

I take in the scene down the sight of my pistol. An open living room/dining room. A woman standing by the dining table. Sobbing. Hysterical. In a T-shirt and panties. Clinging to each leg, terrified, snot faced rugrats stare bug eyed at me.

No, past me.

My blood runs cold. Things go very slow. I hear the click as my head turns. The sliding sound of a semi automatic pistol being cocked. My own gun pointing the wrong fucking way. My head snapping round. Upper body turning as well. Too slow. Too little. Too late. The gun floats into focus. A big one, Glock or a Desert Eagle. The barrel like a huge black sightless eye.

I look up the sights. Right into the eye of a terrified, angry, desperate man. His finger already adding that last crucial pound per square inch. I want to say no. Please don't. In that moment I want to live so bad. I am too slow and it is too late.

He pulls the trigger.

He is less than ten feet away when the gun pointed right at my head goes off. The noise of the explosion is deafening. I watch the top of the barrel slide back as the bullet fires. I see the flash as the powder ignites. I have time to wonder if I will see the slug leave the barrel before it hits me. The barrel is still sliding, moving backwards. Disengaging from the rest of the gun. Exploding. The eye of my killer doesn't have time to change to surprise before it is obliterated by the lump of hot metal. His head snaps back against the wall. His legs give. He slides down, dead before his ass hits the floor. All I can do is stand there, gun pointed at him, staring, beyond disbelief, beyond shock, in some numb other world, a ghost, as Jackson bursts in yelling questions, checking out the woman and the kids, calling for backup, CSI, ambulance.

They called it shock. Put me in overnight for observation. That was all it took. The pill they gave me got me through the night, but no power on earth could stop the DTs from hitting in the morning. Just like that, I was done.

There was plenty of sympathy. Shrinks. But word was out, and by then I'd just had enough. I didn't want to get better. I just wanted to drink enough so that I wouldn't see Fred's tongue working his teeth through that hole in his face. The gun exploding in the apartment. Andy lying in a pool of his own blood.

It should have been me. That's the beginning and the end of it. It should have been me. Would have been me. Andy was great and Fred was a jerk and the restraining order violator was a piece of shit, but none of that matters.

It should have been me.

I know that now. As sure as I know that the end isn't going to be found in the bottom of this bottle.

I'm going to use the .44 I bought for Janie. She left it behind when she walked. It just feels right. Plus I'm sure that the bullet will fit just fine. Feels like it's just been waiting for this moment. The years between, just one bad dream.

I'm done dreaming now.

I know you're scared, but you have to stop crying. I mean it. I want to take my hand off your mouth, but I'm not going to until you stop.

We're in the supply cupboard. I know you can't see anything with the door shut, but trust me, we're safe.

As long as we stay quiet, we're safe.

Shh! Shh, it's okay, it's just thunder. A summer storm.

It's Jesse, right? Jesse, I'm Sam. I work in Mr. Phillips' class. I help Ellis. You know Ellis? Yes, in the wheelchair, right. Just whisper, okay? I will hear you. No, I don't know where he is. Once the... once it started, I just grabbed you and ran. Did you see...? Oh, that's all right, that's normal, the shaking will pass, here, I've got you. It's a reaction. Let's talk about something else.

I know you want Mummy and Daddy. Shh, I know. I'm sure they want you too. You know this is a very special school, right? They must love you very much to send you here. Yes, rich too, sure, of course. Well, because they want the best for you, and they can afford it. No, we have to stay here for now. Because it's not safe. No, don't cry, don't... oh! Let's do story time. Would you like that?

Okay, great! It'll be just like camping out. Have you ever camped out? Well, when people camp out, they stay up late, and sometimes there's a fire, but always, when it's dark, they tell stories. So I'll tell you a story while we wait for the police to come, okay?

Okay.

Do you know the story of the Pied Piper? Right, so you remember how, at the end of the story, he led all the children through a hole in the mountain, and they followed him in there? Well, this story is about what happened next, with those children, okay?

Okay. So. the children stepped into the cave... and gasped with wonder. Inside the mountain, under the ground, was a huge gate, and behind it was another world. There were green, rolling hills, and fields with streams running through them. The sun was bright and warm, and a gentle sweet breeze blew in the faces of the children, ruffling their hair and tickling their noses.

The children filed through the gate, spreading out over the field, taking in the green grass and the fruit-laden trees on the banks of the river. As they smiled at each other, and breathed in through their noses, taking the sweet air into their lungs, the piper quietly shut the gates, before clapping his hands together to get their attention.

The children all turned around to look at him. They remembered the beautiful music he'd played, and how they'd danced for him as they followed him here. It made them feel full of happiness, and they all smiled.

"Now, children," he said, with a voice that sounded like singing, "I have brought you to your new home. My home. The Land of Eternal Sunshine."

He turned to each of the children as he spoke, looking into their eyes. His eyes sparkled gold, looked laughing and kindly. "My home is now your home. Down here, the sun is always warm enough to play, but never so hot as to burn. The breeze will keep you cool but never give you a chill. The water in the rivers and streams are clear and delicious and safe to drink, and the fruit on the trees will fill you up but never give you belly ache. There's no school, ever," (the children cheered at that, as you might guess), "no, bedtime, and no need to sleep – though you can nap under a tree whenever you want. There are no fences or walls. Explore and play to your heart's content."

The children could hardly believe their ears! They jumped for joy, hugging each other and laughing. Then they ran off in all directions – some playing games, others running down to the stream to drink or swim, yet more swarming over the trees, clambering up the trunks, swinging from the branches, or picking and eating the fruit. The trees were huge, and seemed to grow all kinds of fruits, with each child finding their favourite on one branch or another.

Shh! It's just more thunder. A summer storm. It'll pass. Stay with me. Stay with the story.

The children ran and played and lived happily, under the sun that never set or rose.

They ate when they were hungry, napped when they were tired, and played the rest of the time. Whatever they wanted, they seemed to find with little difficulty – art supplies under a rock, board games in a drawer that was built into a tree trunk, somehow. Whatever they could think of to play with, the land provided it. This was before iPads and Playstations and televisions - in the olden days, you must remember. The piper was there too, often just watching and smiling, but sometimes he'd join in the games, dancing, running, and playing his pipes – and when that happened, all the children would join the dance, and leap about together until the tune stopped, when they would all collapse in the grass, panting and laughing.

Anyway. The children were all happy... except for one. There was one child, called Jesse, who... Yes, the same as you!

Jesse – who now I think about it, looked a lot like you, too – was sad. At first, Jesse had been happy enough to play with the other children, helping to build a treehouse and playing with a doll house, but gradually Jesse started to think about Mum and Dad, and to miss them. Once, when wondering in the woods alone, Jesse found a house that looked just like home. Jesse ran in, excited, calling out for Mum and Dad, but the house was empty of people. Jesse went into the old bedroom, and slept in there for a while, but even though the room looked and smelled the same, the sun never went from the window, and there was no noise from the rest of the house, even though back home it was full of the sounds of Mum and Dad and Grandpa talking and laughing and arguing.

Jesse missed them. Jesse also missed the dark. Jesse remembered lying in bed at night, reading books after bedtime. Now, Jesse could read those books anytime – but without the dark, and knowing it was sort-of not allowed, Jesse didn't want to anymore.

Jesse missed home.

So Jesse went to talk to The Piper.

Jesse found him sitting under the shade of a tree, by the banks of the stream. The Piper was watching a big group of children playing ring-a-rosie, with a small smile on his face. Next to him, a fishing rod was on a stand over the stream. Jesse watched the red float on the end of the string moving up and down in the water for a long time, trying to feel brave enough to speak.

Hoping The Piper would speak first, or even just look over.

But he didn't. So eventually, Jesse spoke up.

"Mr. Piper?"

The Piper turned to look at Jesse. His face was still smiling, and the golden flecks in his eyes still danced, but Jesse thought he looked tired, suddenly. Tired, and old, and sad.

He looked, but didn't speak. Jesse coughed, then spoke again.

"Mr. Piper... I miss my mum and dad. I miss home."

The Pipers' smile got wider at that, but Jesse could see clearly that it was a very sad smile.

The Piper nodded, gently.

"Piper, I... I want to go home. I need to."

At first Jesse thought The Piper wasn't going to reply at all, only keep smiling his sad smile, but finally he did, looking away from Jesse and over to the horizon as he did so.

"I know you feel that way, Jesse. I feel it. The land feels it. That's why we made you the house."

"We?"

"The land and I are one. We exist to serve you and make you happy."

"But I can't be happy without my parents."

The Piper sighed. "Your parents are the reason you are here. Surely you know this?"

Jesse frowned at this, unsure what The Piper meant. "I know they made me..."

The Piper shook his head, eyes still on the horizon. "I mean, the reason you're here with me. Jesse, I saved your town. Do you not recall?"

Jesse did. Jesse remembered the rats, the food shortages, the disease, the fear. Remembered, too, the Piper's extraordinary claims, and still more extraordinary deed, the sight of the rats dancing their way into the river. Jesse remembered them dancing even as they drowned, and the memory made Jesse shiver.

The Piper continued, as if Jesse had answered. "And you recall, do you not, that all I asked in return was to be paid fair for my work, and how the townsfolk refused me?"

Jesse remembered hearing the grownups discussing it behind closed doors. There had been disagreements, but the settled view emerged pretty quickly.

"The rats had destroyed so much! Paying you what you asked would have made things harder..."

The Piper turned back, and for the first time, Jesse saw no smile at all on his kind face.

"Hard, Jesse? Hard compared to what?"

Jesse had no reply.

"They made their choice. They must live with the consequence."

"But it's not fair!" Jesse blurted out.

Shh! Yes, it's getting close. No, you're right, it's not thunder. Stay with the story.

Jesse said "It's not my fault they made a bad decision. I don't deserve to suffer for it."

The Piper sighed. "How do you suffer, Jesse? You're here, in The Land of Eternal Sunshine. None of the other children are sad. See how they play and laugh." The Piper swept his arm across the landscape, at the children laughing and playing and skipping and sitting and napping. "It's no punishment for them – for you. You're free – free to live as children should, and free to never have to grow up or grow old. Here you are safe and loved – by me and the by the land."

Jesse looked inside and saw that it was true. Jesse did feel loved, did feel safe. The land was beautiful, and kind. But still...

"Still, I miss them. I want them back."

The Piper finally turned back to Jesse. There were tears in his eyes.

"You wish to return?"

"Is there... Can I? Is it possible?"

Jesse's breath held, waiting for the answer. The Piper's sad, wide eyes took Jesse in. And suddenly Jesse understood.

Do you understand, Jesse? Debts have to be paid. We're in here! Debts have to be paid, and sometimes the debts of parents are paid by their children, and it's not fair, but it's all there is. Sometimes parents do bad things, and hurt people. Sometimes they think they can do things, or take things, without having to pay for them. Sometimes, they get so rich they forget that they have to.

But they always do. In the end, everyone pays, one way or another.

It'll all be over in a second.

Don't look at the gun.

All Loving, All Knowing

Thirty seconds before he took the knife from his kitchen into his living room and stabbed his wife and daughter to death, proceeding thence to open his own throat with the same blade, Benjamin Swindon would have told you he was entirely calm.

He wasn't, of course. Whilst genuinely cold-blooded murder does happen from time to time, even with so-called loved ones, it's a relatively rare beast, in my long experience. In truth, what happened in those thirty seconds was the product of a lifetime and more of bad decisions made, mainly by men with the surname Swindon, most assuredly including young Benjamin – and oh, sure the odd dose of bad luck, too.

Let's take a closer look, shall we?

Benji (as his wife, Katie, insisted on calling him, especially when she was in a teasing mood, which she often was, imagining his exasperation was put on rather than genuine, this misunderstanding based on behavior she had seen modeled as a child, when her own mother would frequently tease her father by calling him Teddy, and he would respond with a mock growl but then throw her a wink to let her know he wasn't really mad [and the memory that she's blanked because she was too young, of being woken by the sound of her mother calling him Teddy in *that* voice, and then the sound of rustling and moaning, her mother's voice raised in pleasure], and sometimes when she calls him Benji she feels a flutter without quite knowing why, which is part of why she does it so much, misreading his genuine frustration as fake and flirtatious, just keeping things spicy) is cleaning what his mind *insists* on calling the George Formby grill, thanks to Katie's Peter Kay addiction (Benji is half convinced Katie is actually a bit sweet on Kay, and he's not wrong – on more than one occasion, Katie has brought herself to climax in a sneaky afternoon rampant rabbit session imagining Mr. Kay's cheeky smile looking down at her in the mirror as he bends her over a dressing table, and once she tried to imagine Benji was Kay when they were having sex, but it made her feel sad, so she didn't do it again). He's cleaning the grill because he's been tasked with making Sunday morning brunch – i.e. bacon sarnies – his bitter festering resentment at this task, at the *assumption* that Just Because It's Sunday He Has To Cook being out of all proportion to the scale of the task; which is, after all, the only day of the week he has to prepare food, and that preparation consisting entirely of grilling seven rashers of bacon, and toasting two slices of bread, and buttering three other slices of bread, and adding ketchup to one of them.

But resent the task, bitterly and festeringly, he *does*, and though he doesn't consciously realise it, this current exercise is a big part of why; it's the cleaning the grill that so infuriates him, and he doesn't know that (consciously), and because he doesn't know that (consciously), he doesn't know *why*, doesn't realise it's because his own mother always taught him to wash up once the cooking and eating was done, and he'd always done this, even as an otherwise utter slob of a teenager and young adult, he'd *always*, no matter how filthy his surroundings, washed up his plates and cutlery and cooking pots and pans after every single meal and Katie didn't. She left meat tins, just put them back in the oven, where they festered all week until they were needed, at which point she (or, more often, *Benji*) ended up washing them up, and he *hates* it, and he pretends he hates it because the point of washing up after you use it is that it's clean when you need to use it again the next time. And he really thinks that's the root of it, the beginning and end, he can't imagine – literally is incapable of the feat of imagination needed to comprehend – that the simple truth is it goes against what his mother taught him.

And if you're asking yourself why Benji doesn't merely clean the grill after he's eaten brunch each Sunday, and for that matter why the lazy little shit doesn't also wash up the meat tins after his wife has cooked a Sunday roast (and I know that you are), you're doing a pretty good job of demonstrating why you're very unlikely to murder your spouse and child thirty seconds after beginning to clean a George Foreman grill.

So. Benji is cleaning the grill, and all of this is swirling around, in the underneath part of his brain where all the really groovy human stuff actually happens, and beyond some screamingly strong feelings he thinks are faint because he doesn't understand how any of this shit works, he watches his fingers rubbing the dishcloth that's scraping away last week's dried-on bacon fat, the white streaks that look to Benji like dripping cum, and which release the scent of rancid bacon as he wipes away at them, a smell infuriating because it's so close to something good that it offends with its proximity to greatness – like a really shitty cover of a magnificent song – and as the dirty water runs down into the drip tray which he's forgotten is cracked at one end and needs propping up or the fat from the grill ends up all over the surface of the counter and on the floor where he'll have to fucking clean it up *again*, and if Katie sees he's forgotten *again* she'll look at him cleaning and *laugh*, actually *laugh* at him on his hands and knees *cleaning* (and if you think from this that our man Benji here has some pretty deep seated issues around women that he's barely acknowledged, well, no duh, and if you're starting to wonder if he'd still have committed a double homicide if his kid had been a boy, award yourself a gold star, but don't think that means your own shit doesn't stink, because I've smelt it, and it most assuredly does). As he cleans, sacrilegious smell of rancid bacon in his nostrils, drip tray seventeen seconds away from spilling out the filthy water and rancid fat onto the counter, nineteen seconds away from his sleeve catching a glass on the side as he turns to grab a dishcloth to stop up the spill, twenty seconds away from that glass shattering at his feet, causing him to jump back and, at twenty and a half seconds, catch the edge of the drip tray with his other hand as he does so, causing it to flip into the air towards him, spraying his face with lukewarm rancid bacon fat water, twenty one seconds before *that* bullshit causes him to take a half step back, painfully puncturing the sole of his foot on the broken gin glass he'd bought his wife for Christmas – her favourite glass, and one of two, the other of which he'd broken exactly seven months before and which had really upset her, even though she'd shrugged it off to him, and she'd pretended it didn't bother her and he'd believed it didn't, but deep down he'd known he'd disappointed her again (all this happening down below, where shit is *always* real and the lies never fly), twenty four seconds before three seconds of blinking have just made his eyes sting even worse, twenty six seconds before his hand closes around the handle of the super sharp carving knife in the second drawer and he thinks, at twenty seven seconds, his last fully lucid, coherent thought (which is, of course, *fuck it*), and twenty nine seconds before, having taken a deep, even breath, he turns to leave the kitchen, knife in hand, to go into the living room, there to stab Katie to death in front of his screaming, hysterical daughter, seven savage punches to the chest, aiming for the heart, pranging the blade on ribs on the first three attempts but making it through with the other four, the fifth blow being strong enough to puncture clean through her entire body (meaning that her left lung was punctured back and front, and even if he hadn't pierced her heart, she'd have drowned in her own blood within ten minutes), before taking the blade to his still hysterical child, whose high pitched screams only cease when he drives the knife straight through her in a single blow, the light in her eyes sparking out even before the blood erupts from her mouth and dribbles down her chin, and, tearing the blade from her with a grunt of effort, without stopping to survey the charnel house he's converted his very ordinary living room into, calmly turning the knife around and slitting his own throat.

What he's thinking, twenty nine seconds before all that, in a dull, vaguely hungover way, is the word *respect*. And in the back of his mind, he hears Mick Jagger sing *I'm not your Beast of Burden*, and he smiles what he imagines is a rueful smile, but one which is actually full of violent hatred.

And that's how it happens. That's how it always happens, basically. The Boomtown Rats were not far off.

Oh, really? *That's* your question?

Yeah, I know. You can't help asking. Design flaw. My bad.

Because, as nobody knew, and no one will ever know, given the clear cause of death and no desire to inflict a detailed autopsy on a seven year old child, Benji's daughter had an inoperable brain tumor, the symptoms of which would have started manifesting within the week, and which would have killed her, after a great deal of pain and invasive but ultimately futile surgery, exactly three months later. The death would have devastated Katie, who would have taken her own life, and Benji... well, actually Benji would just have used it as an excuse to go full blown alcoholic and sleep with an eye watering number of sex workers, and he'd have been secretly quite happy with how his life turned out – which is why I was quite happy to see things play out the way they did. This way, mother and daughter live in my eternal light and grace, and Benji... well, he got to where he was going anyway – just a little quicker, and having done, in toto, a lot less harm.

So, yes, that's why I sent the word *respect* into his mind, at precisely that moment. Because that's all it ever takes – a tiny nudge at the right time, and it's happily ever after, in this, the best of all possible worlds.

You're welcome.

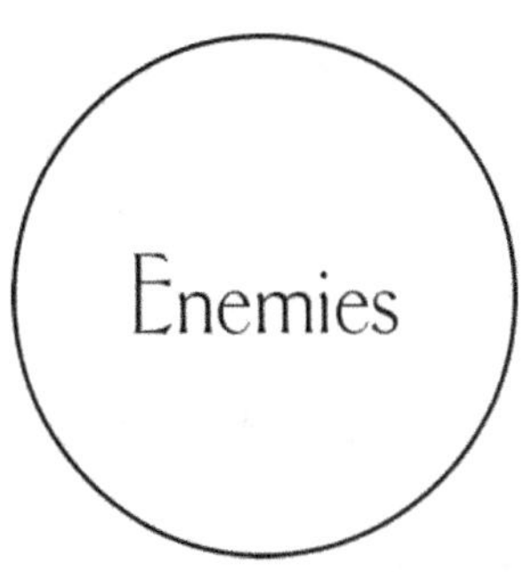

Enemies

The mist swirls around me. No, fog. It's thick, chilly. It clings to my coat, leaving beads of moisture like tiny glistening eggs on the woolly fibres.

It's dark. The world is grey and I can't make out a light source, but I can see a short distance ahead and behind. It's like being inside a ten-foot dome. Beyond, that grey wall of gently-writhing water vapour.

My hands ache with the cold. I push them deep into my jacket pockets, hunching my shoulders. The air is thick enough that each inhalation feels damp as well as chilling, cold enough that I see my breath join with the mist on each exhale.

I'm moving forward. I feel the cold through my trousers, but oddly the damp cloth doesn't seem to chill my skin.

I'm headed somewhere. There's a definite directional pull. My mind pulls up an image of a needle in a compass, swinging back to north.

I keep walking. I'll know it when I see it.

The ground is even but not slippery, despite the moisture in the air. My boots grip with ease. My toes are warm inside fluffy socks.

I can't remember how I got here. I walk and try to think, but the swirling nature of the fog keeps throwing up half-shapes and figures to distract me, and my curiosity keeps trying to pivot to where, exactly, the light is coming from; how it can be all about with no clear source. Maybe it's not an external source. Maybe the fog...

Then I hear a sound from up ahead. It's a tapping, knocking sound. Wood on wood. My temperature doesn't change, but I shiver just the same. It's a heavy sound, pregnant even. *What foul beast*, I half think, and shudder again. But there's no doubt – the noise is dead ahead.

My destination.

I feel foreboding bloom in my chest, spreading throughout my body, like there's a lump of ice in my heart suddenly, pumping a numbing dread through my whole system.

My feet keep moving. My boots rise and fall. The quality of my footsteps changes. The sound of each footfall becomes hollow, echoey, and underneath that, I begin to become aware of an organic, slapping sound. My mind conjures an image of damp corpse hands, clapping together in some arrhythmic applause. My scalp prickles. I smell decay, brine, and just as I picture the hands rising, perhaps gripping my ankle to pull me into the ground, my mind makes the connection between sound and smell: I'm on a pier.

It helps, a bit. The corpse hands become the waves they always were, lapping against the supports of the platform I must be on – as if on cue, the wood creaks beneath my feet – but the water is cold and black and very deep, poisoned with salt. In my mind I see tentacles, bone-white and massive, pushing up from the deep (razor sharp suckers designed to rend flesh, sharp enough to cut bone and strong enough to suck marrow), rising towards the hated dim glow overhead; the rickety structure that sticks out like a crude finger over the realm of...

There's a light ahead. It's a flame, I think. There's an orange tinge to it, and it flickers and dances. It's directly in front of me. In my way. I know beyond doubt that this flame is what is pulling me forwards. Part of me is comforted. After all, it's a real light as opposed to this amorphous glow I'm currently surrounded by. Flame offers the chance of heat, and company.

Of course, under the circumstances, company is pretty well the definition of a double-edged sword. I move forward anyway, legs on automatic. The wood beneath me creaks more often, and the waves sound closer – surely an illusion, some kind of auditory mirage? The light grows, resolving to a single bright flame. I find it hard to credit that anything could burn so bright in this air, but the fire stands tall in defiance of the atmosphere. It appears to create a halo of clear air around it, burning the fog away.

The flame is flickering some seven feet above the ground. As I draw closer, the glow it casts illuminates the wooden floor. Rough planking, warped with age, rickety. The platform is perhaps ten feet wide. Beyond that, perfect darkness and the aroma of salt.

Beneath the flame, a figure appears, emerging as though being birthed from the fog itself, or perhaps formed *of* it. He is tall, over six foot, and in his right fist he holds the flaming torch aloft. The light is bright yellow and billows around the lumpen end of the handle, like some out-sized juggling prop. The smoke is thick and black, rising a few feet before being absorbed by the grey air.

The hand that grips the handle is large and gnarled. The flame flickers and rolls, strobing over his pale, grubby knuckles. The arm that raises the fist is scrawny but thick. Muscles show under dirty, leathery skin. My gaze moves to his bare shoulder, rounded and powerful. His robe is made of a coarse dark cloth, held at the waist with a thick rope belt. The hood is down, lying crumpled around his neck.

My feet carry me inexorably forward as his face swims into focus. His features are aged, weathered, but his eyes are still vital, almost wild. They stare aggressively from underneath dark-grey brows, bushy and tangled. His forehead is very high, but long messy braids of black hair lie about his neck, spilling either side of his face. His nose is large and misshapen, as if by injury or disease. His mouth is set in a frown, above an imposing, jutting chin.

My boots step towards him with an inexorable, unbroken rhythm. As I take him in, I feel a resonance within. I still understand very little about where I am, or why, but I suddenly intuit much. It's a deeply unsettling feeling.

I stop, roughly ten feet from the figure. Rather, my legs stop moving. We regard each other.

'You know who I am.' His voice is deep and cracked and resonant.

'Actually, I...'

'You know who I am.' It's not a question, I realise. With dismay, I also realise the truth of the statement.

'Yes.'

He nods. The torch moves from one hand to the other, and he holds it out over the edge of the pier. The yellow flame ripples, bathing a crude wooden rowing boat with flickering light.

'You will cross with me. Soon.'

I nod, feeling my eyes itching, my throat contracting. I'm scared. I'm also sad.

'But first...'

He lowers the torch, igniting an iron brazier filled with logs (which I could almost swear wasn't there a moment ago). The twisted, dry wood almost explodes into flame. I flinch, and the heat is uncomfortable on my exposed face, almost painful, but I do not move back.

'...first, you face your enemies.'

I feel sweaty, and the sudden flame is only part of the reason. My stomach tightens.

'You have questions.'

'I—yes.'

'I will allow you to ask three.'

'Why is it always three?' It's out before I can stop it. But honestly, I've always wanted to know.

'Because it always is.'

His face doesn't change, but I swear that I see something flicker in his eyes – some cold amusement, or contempt. He holds up his free hand, palm out, little finger held under his thumb. Then he lowers his ring finger also.

Two left.

I curse myself. My mind swirls. So many questions...but it seems like there's only one that really matters.

'I have to fight my enemies now?'

'No.'

'Then what?'

'You have to decide.'

'Decide what?'

He is silent. His eyes look to his now closed fist, then back to my face.

No more questions.

He gestures at the brazier. The flame roars higher, and as it dies down, a figure steps out from behind it. It's a boy, an infant. Dark bowl haircut, a T-shirt and jeans. He's handsome. A little chubby. I'm hit with a dizzying sense of recognition, but I cannot place him. It's maddening. He stares at me, expression blank, apparently unaffected by the heat of the naked flames.

'Your first enemy. Tom Callum.'

The name is like a boot to the door of my memory, throwing light into a room I haven't even been near in...too long. Forever.

'Tom...' Remembering cowboys and Indians. Remembering cops and robbers. Stealing from a packed-lunch box in the cloak room. Blowing bubbles through a straw into milk, but...

'Tom wasn't my enemy! We were friends. He was my—' *my first best friend*, I think, but the figure is shaking his head.

'Tom was a bad friend. He disliked you. He used you to make himself feel better. You proved to him that he could get people to like him, and that's all you were to him. He treated you like his dog and thought of you like an insect.'

The words cut. The truth of them cuts. Still...

'He was a kid, I was a kid. I didn't know any of that, so where's the harm?'

The figure shrugs, an expression of elemental indifference. 'Tell me your choice.'

'My choice? What choice?'

He looks me in the eyes then, full bore, those dark eyes pinning me like a bug to a windscreen.

'Forgive or condemn?'

His eyes still hold me. I want to shake my head to clear it, but I can't look away. 'What difference does it make? What does my choice mean?'

His eyes leave mine, turning back to his closed fist. The answer is clear.

No more questions.

I shrug, and a shaky laugh comes out of me.

'OK, fine, fuck it, forgive. He was a boy, I don't care.'

The figure nods once. The fire roars, and the boy vanishes. As the flame lowers, another figure steps around the fire, the opposite side to where the boy had stood.

An older boy. Fat-faced. A small cluster of dark moles under his left nostril. Pasty white skin. My breath catches in my throat, and I feel a mini adrenaline spike. The last time I saw that face...

'Your second enemy. Stephen...'

'I know who he is. I know what he did.'

For a moment I think the figure is going to read out the crime sheet anyway, like he doesn't have a choice but, for a mercy, he stays silent. Still, I smell blood; remember the taste of my own tears.

'Forgive or condemn?'

I feel my stomach roil, anger and dread. But he was just a boy, just a child, just young, just spoiled; not his fault. Then I remember his fists in my stomach, the look in his face. I remember feeling hate for the first time.

'Fuck him.'

I think the figure is going to get officious, demand the correct language, but he just nods again. The boy's expression does not change, and the fire roars, driving needles of heat and too-bright light into my eyes. I screw them shut reflexively, and when I open them again, Stephen is gone.

And so it goes. The enemies come, I pass judgment; they go. My first boss (forgiven), my first boyfriend (forgiven), my first boyfriend's girlfriend's sister (condemned), two more 'best friends' (condemned, both), strangers I never knew had hated me and harmed me, ex-lovers and ex-colleagues – and I forgive, forgive, forgive. I've lost track of time, of numbers.

The fire flares. I close my eyes, and when I open them, Sarah is there.

She's wearing the white nightdress she wore for so many years of our marriage. Her long black hair falls free, down to her waist, curling there. Her face is older than when we met, more careworn, but still striking, handsome, beautiful. No make-up. She stares ahead, blankly.

'I don't understand.'

'Sarah Locke.'

'I know who she is, I know my wife! But why...'

'She held you back.'

The accusation floors me completely.

'She feared you, and sought to control you because of her fear. She learned to hide her fear, and the loathing underneath that fear, but she held you back. Kept you from fulfilling your true potential. Clipped your wings, your ambitions; held you in place—'

'No! No, she loved me, she...'

'She loved you. She feared you. She loathed you. She held you in place. She held you back.'

My eyes scan her face, looking for some note of confirmation or denial, but her features don't change, and I realise that she's not really here at all. I'm looking at a waxwork model, a replica. Instead, I reach within, and feel...

I feel resonance. It's awful, but I feel truth. I remember now, sleepless nights. I remember too, nights when the dreams came, dark and terrible, fading as I woke. I remember awaking with a feeling of dread crushing my chest.

It's true. He speaks truth. Something in her had tried to control me, hold me back, and yet...

'She loved me.'

Silence.

'Forgiven.'

I close my eyes as the fire flares. I don't want to see her go.

I open my eyes, already looking to the other side of the fire, wondering how many more I have to see, how many...

My thoughts freeze. The thing standing in front of me is enormous – maybe eight-feet tall – hulking, broad. It wears a brown felt hat, like a fedora. The brim is pulled low, but the crescent shadow cannot fully conceal the fact that the creature has no nose. There are flickering pinpricks of reflected firelight in that shadow, where eyes would be. Below, there is grey-pink flesh; lumpen, glistening slightly, as though coated in some translucent fluid. The jaw is almost cartoonish in length, chin jutting; an obscenity. Above sits the mouth, a lipless hole filled with black, pointed teeth, jagged and jumbled like that of a shark.

An ankle-length trench coat and large black boots cover the rest of the thing from view, except for one final detail: the hand-sized scalpel blades which protrude from the sleeves of the coat.

My sweat seems to turn chill in a second and, despite the heat of the fire, I shudder.

'Your penultimate enemy. The Teacher.'

'The...what the *fuck* is that?' I'm whispering, terrified that the figure will move, come to life, attack with those blades or those awful teeth.

'The Teacher.'

'I don't...I mean, I never...'

'No. You would remember.'

My nerves are jagged and raw, but I could still almost swear that was a joke. Maybe. 'Nonetheless, it was your enemy.'

'Why? How?'

'It hunts your kind. You had come to its attention, and it was on its way to you. Had it found you, it would have destroyed you.'

I take in the shape, mind not quite able to accept the physical fact of it, rebelling at the notion of this thing as real, even as the firelight bathes it in a yellow glow. *Your kind*...the phrase is like a bucket of cold water to the face. I feel mortal dread rise in me.

'I don't, I can't—'

'No. But you need only decide.'

I stare at it a little while longer. It meant my destruction, but I never saw it. The teeth, those blades...

'No. Condemn.'

The figure nods, the flame rises, the monster fades from view.

On the other side of the fire—

'Your final enemy. Your mortal enemy.'

He's exactly as I remember, the last time I

saw him. I know this for sure, even as I realise I'm incapable of remembering that last sight, the last time we stood face to face. It's terrifying, the realisation of that; the implications. I feel my mind reeling, like some mooring is coming loose, a terrible strain on the roots of my thoughts, like something is being torn.

'Jacob Locke.'

'Son.' The word comes out as a sob. I'm aware I've spoken aloud, but it's as though it's happening to someone else, being reported to me through wires over some terrible distance. I float in a void, and across the darkness I feel my eyes move in their sockets, picking out the shape of my son's teenage face, lit by fire. Still some of that chubbiness about the face, even as the fur is starting to show on his upper lip. Those beautiful blue eyes. That brow, so quick to furrow when upset or angry, one of my gifts to him. Ah, Son, why are you here? I feel my eyes move again, taking in his frame, his clothes, T-shirt, shorts, white trainers. His T-shirt is stained, dark fluid on the yellow fabric. His left arm is also darkened. I start to feel a burning pain in my lower back. His fist is clenched. Another pain, higher. His fist is black, dripping with dark fluid. More pain now, in my side, upper back, I should be falling, but the pain is both real and unreal, there and not there.

Like him.

Like me.

I look up at the figure, aware that there are tears running down my face now. I feel pain, and a throbbing rage, dark and terrible, choking me.

He stares back, impassive.

'Make your last choice. Make it, and we will be on our way.'

I look back to my son. I see him, and there's a doubling in my mind; he is my son, he is meat; I love him, I despise him; I am repulsed by him, I am repulsed by myself; I want...

'What happened?'

Nothing.

I want...

'WHAT AM I?'

Nothing.

I lower my head. The tears run down my nose, fall to the ground.

'I forgive.'

I feel the fire flare. I do not look up. It roars, high and bright and fierce, then dies away to a red glow. Only coals now, soon to fade entirely, red to grey to black.

Dying.

'It's time.'

I look up. The figure is already in the boat, reaching his hand out to me.

I take a step forwards, then stop.

'There's a price, isn't there?'

He looks back, and for a moment, I think he isn't going to answer.

'There's always a price.'

'Okay. But I'm not even going to discuss that until you get me across. Clear?'

He nods, solemn.

I take his hand, and step into the boat.

It's so good to finally see another person! This is so exciting! Hi, how are you, I'm William, pleased to meet you, it's okay, I won't try and touch you, I can see you look poorly, you just sit there, that's fine.

This is so great! It's just been me for, gosh, I don't even know how long. Harry, that's who brought you in, well, I call him Harry, I don't really know his name but he looks like a Harry I think, anyway Harry only comes in if I'm doing something wrong or if they're taking me away for an operation and he never says anything, so...

But it's nice here, though. They've got all the Sky channels on the TV! Well, all the kids ones, plus the superhero movies. And the Playstation! I love Playstation, do you?

Can you nod, or...? Okay, never mind, don't worry.

Anyway, yeah, it's great, the beds are nice and big and you can eat what you want, there's always food in the fridge and the phone, well, you can say what you want to eat, if it's not in the fridge and they send it up, there's a special cupboard over there, well, it's like a lift for food, anyway you can get what you want. I have pizza a lot. I like pizza.

The only downer is the water. It's all there is to drink and it tastes a bit funny. I miss cola and lemonade, but it's okay I guess. And we have straws, so, you know, you'll be okay.

Anyway, there's another room that I don't use, so I guess you can have that. I wonder why they've put you in here! Maybe when you're feeling better, you can... well, maybe write down your name, or something?

Sorry, never mind. Hey, so I can tell you about me! I'm William, and I think I must be nine or ten. I forget exactly. The Superhero channel turns into the christmas channel for a month every year, but I'm not sure how many times that's happened since I got here. That sounds so silly, doesn't it? At least twice, but is it three or four, I just honestly can't remember. It's always the same movies, that's the problem. I'm sure I'd remember if there were new ones, probably...

Anyway I was seven when I came here. I had to. I'd killed both my parents.

I didn't mean to! It was an accident.

I killed my mum when I was six. I'd had a wobbly tooth for ages, my front one, I mean. I remember flicking it with my tongue, how it felt. It felt nice. It made the girls scream in the playground when I did it, and some of the boys too, and Miss Elmer said I had to stop doing it in class because it was a distraction so I shut my mouth but I kept doing it. It felt... I can't really explain it, but it felt *really* good, like when you're waiting to get on a ride at the funfair, and you *know* it's going to be really exciting, and just the waiting becomes exciting? It was like that.

Flick, flick, flick, all the time, it felt looser and looser but it wouldn't come out. It got so I could even twist it around with just my tongue, and mum said it would come out any day, but it stayed that way for a week and it still wasn't coming out, but I didn't care. I liked the feeling, and I didn't want it to go; didn't really want the tooth to fall out. But I couldn't stop playing with it.

And then one break I was playing frisbees with Angus, and we'd been going back and forth, seeing how many times we could pass it without dropping it, but also how fast we could throw it back, and I'd just thrown it fast but a bit high, and he jumped to catch it and threw it straight back while he was still in the air and it went *really fast* and it hit me right in the mouth.

It all happened super quick. I felt a click that was like a crunch, and *right as it happened* I thought about my mum saying 'that tooth'll come out any day', I actually pictured her saying it as the tooth snapped off in my mouth. I felt something click in my head, too, at that exact moment. The snap of the tooth and the click in my mind and the image of my mum.

I was most of the way through the afternoon class when the head teacher came in and took me into her office. I knew I wasn't in trouble because I hadn't done anything but I didn't know what it *was* about, and then she told me that my mum was dead and I knew why straight away, and I cried because I knew I'd done it, all at once, I knew the click had meant something and I hadn't known what but now I did and I wanted to take it back but I couldn't, but she didn't know that was why I was crying, so *that* was okay. Because I suppose it's normal to cry when you find out your mum died even if you didn't kill her.

Anyway, so that's how I killed my mum. They tried to tell me it was something called an embolism, but I knew better. And I was home from school for a while, and dad was very sad, really sad, and there was a funeral and stuff, and I was sad and I missed her but honestly the worst part was that I couldn't tell anyone it was my fault. I mean, I did say it, but people kept telling me that I mussent say it, that it wasn't true, and even though it was, people got so angry and upset that I stopped saying it, but I thought it.

And then I started getting another wobbly tooth.

It was the one next to it, my other front tooth. I felt it move when I bit into an apple and feeling it made me drop the apple and burst into tears, but my dad who was there thought I was just crying because I was sad so he hugged me and didn't ask, so *that* was okay, but I was scared.

I stopped eating hard foods; anything that I needed my front teeth for, I, you know, tried to chew in from the side, and people thought I looked funny, other kids, they would stare and not laugh because everyone knew about my mum and had been told not to pick on me, but they looked and looked and it was horrible, but I had to avoid using the tooth so I kept going. There was one girl, she kept staring, a mean stare, I thought, and it made me angry, and I thought that I'd just think of her and bite into a Granny Smith and that'd teach her a lesson, and then I'd feel awful for thinking it, and carry on chewing with the side of my mouth.

I tried making a list of mean people. I knew it was going to happen, the tooth had to come out eventually, so I tried to think of people I really didn't like but there were mean kids and teachers who'd been a bit unfair but I couldn't think of anyone who deserved to die. The worst part was I was scared that it'd happen and I'd think of Dad and he'd die as well. And have you ever tried to not think about someone? It's really hard, your mind keeps going to where you don't want it.

I hoped it would fall out in my sleep, when I

wasn't thinking about anything, that I'd wake up with the tooth on my pillow, but then I had a dream about dad and woke up terrified it had happened, and it hadn't but the tooth was so loose that even just brushing my tongue up against it made it move. It took me ages to get back to sleep again.

I woke up again the morning after the nightmare, and I was feeling sick, I remember that. My dad was frying bacon in the kitchen and I could smell it and I used to love the smell but it seemed like everything made me feel sick, by that time, especially anything food related. I went for a wee and I could hear two voices from the kitchen, the radio man and dad's voice. I couldn't make out what either were talking about but I could hear from dad's tone that he wasn't too happy. Not that he was ever happy after mum, but, you know. Angry, I mean. I finished weeing and forgot to flush and washed my hands and then walked towards the kitchen and gradually the words became more clear. The radio man was talking about immigration and Europe and laws, and as I got to the door I heard my dad yell 'You're an evil cunt!' and I knew who he meant, I'd seen the man, on the posters for his show and on the telly, and my dad always hated him, went on at mum about how evil he was and that, and suddenly I felt okay, like a weight was lifting, and I pictured the man in my head, as clear as if he was standing in front of me, and then I reached into my mouth and tugged the tooth and it was so loose it just popped straight out into my hand, and as it went I felt something, that snapping my mind, and I walked into the room holding up the tooth and said 'look, Dad, my other tooth came out!', and as I said it, the man on the radio had gone silent, and as dad gave me a hug the program on the radio suddenly changed, and then a short while later they announced that the man had died, right in his seat in the middle of his show.

Another embolism.

I hoped it would make dad happy, the man dying, not the tooth, but it didn't, well, neither did. It stayed on the news for nearly a week, the man dying, not the tooth, obviously, and I remember my dad saying 'Ah, who cares about that evil bastard' and turning the radio off, then looking at me and saying sorry. But he wasn't happy, and then the news kept saying the man's party was doing even better and that just made dad more angry. And that meant I was sad, too, but at least I didn't have the guilt the same way I did with mum because the man was evil so at least it was good that he'd died and stopped doing evil things.

But I did have another wobbly tooth.

I started feeling really ill then, all the time. I wasn't hungry and food would give me belly ache and I couldn't sleep at night and couldn't stay awake during the day and it was horrible. It's really funny to me now – I mean I can remember how it felt, like I can remember how sad I was when my mum died, but I don't feel any of that any more; it's like you can remember when you hurt yourself, but it doesn't hurt anymore? Like that. All gone, since I came here.

But yeah, back then, it was horrible. The tooth was all I could think about, lying awake at night. I would feel it there, every time I swallowed, it would *move*, like it *wanted* to fall out, wanted to come loose and have me kill someone. I hated it. Hated myself. I didn't care that it wasn't my fault.

I actually kind of wanted to die. I wondered what would happen if I thought of myself when it happened, if that would work. But then I thought about my dad and how sad he would be. And also I was scared.

Dad had gotten worse, too, I think because I had. He used to be able to make me laugh no matter what, when mum was alive. No matter how cross or sad I'd get, he just knew what to say to make me smile. Mum used to be annoyed by that, or pretend to be, who knows with grown ups. But now he was just so sad, he looked old, I mean, like grandpa old, not just dad old. And he couldn't find the words anymore, or I was too sad for them to work, I don't know. Either way, we'd just sit there, me feeling terrible and him looking terrible. The tooth, one of the front bottom ones, getting looser with each day.

That was a problem, too. Dad had seen it, so loose now it flopped forward in my mouth whenever I opened it, and kept asking me if it had fallen out, if I was going to pull it. I couldn't tell him. I couldn't. And he kept going on about it more and more. I think he knew it's why I was avoiding food that wasn't soft, why I was eating funny.

Then came the night we were watching TV. I don't know if he'd planned it or not, but I guess my loose tooth and funny eating were starting to get to him. Or maybe it was something he just did without thinking. Anyway, that's when he got me. We were watching the final of Britain's Got Talent. Me and Dad had always watched it together, Mum tutting and rolling her eyes, but secretly watching it too, and we hadn't watched it since she died, but it was the final and Dad asked me and I said okay, and we sat there side by side. And there was a man who was doing a trick with a sword, throwing it about and chopping up a melon, and he moved so fast, so strong, and I leaned forward and so did my dad, and he threw the sword super high into the air, and my mouth fell open, and my dad moved super-quick, I barely realised he'd moved at all until I felt the pull and the snap, in my mouth but also in my mind, and the man on the TV fell straight onto the ground. His head banged, and there was blood on his nose, and the sword fell onto the stage with a clang, and then the picture went funny and there was a scream and then it went away, and I looked over at my dad and he was looking at me, the tooth in his hand and his eyes open wide, looking from the TV to me back to the TV, frowning, face turning red, and now he didn't look like a grandpa but a crazy old man, like out of a film, and his breath was bad as he said 'What *are* you?'

I think I could have sat there for a million years. I couldn't think of anything; I don't mean anything to say, I mean anything at all. Then he said "What have you done?" and he grabbed my hand, and his grip was hot and hard, and I jumped up, pulling away, and I stood in the doorway and looked at him, and he looked at the tooth and then back at me, and I could see his face changing, into something I'd never seen before, and as he looked back at the tooth, he said in a quiet, quiet voice 'William, what happened to your mother?' and then he looked back at me, and I saw his eyes, and I ran.

The only thing I still think about now – and I mean it doesn't bother me, I sleep great since I got here, and I don't ever get sad, which is nice – is that I didn't run out of the front door. I wonder about that, why I ran into the bathroom instead. I don't know why I did that.

But I did, and I locked the door, and a short while later, dad started banging on the door, yelling. Not words, just noise. I knew what he was going to do. And I knew what I had to do to stop him.

I was crying. I yelled 'I love you, dad, I'm sorry' and he yelled louder, and I went to the sink, and bit the edge of it, making sure my other lower tooth was resting against it, staring down the plug hole, bent forward, and as I heard the door slam against the wall I hit my jaw as hard as I could. I felt a stab of pain, and tasted blood, but there was no snap, and then I was flying through the air sideways. I hit the wall and slid down it. I remember feeling the hit, but no pain. I looked up and my dad was almost on top of me, lifting me up by the throat. His face was all the way crazy, red. As he lifted me, I put my hand in my mouth and tore at the tooth. It was slippery with blood but I'd hit it hard enough, it really hurt and it made me cry but I ripped it out and as I did I felt the snap in my head, and my dad fell to the floor straight away, letting go of my throat.

I went away for a while after that. There were people in uniforms, and then doctors and nurses. They all kept asking me what had happened. And I told them. I told them all. It just didn't seem to matter much anymore. I don't remember most of it. There was a hospital. They told me I'd had stitches in my mouth. They told me they'd given me something for the pain.

And then I woke up here, with Harry. He told me I'd be taken care of, and that they'd make me feel better, so I wasn't sad anymore. He said they believed me, and they wanted to help me. He seemed nice. They said I could have what I wanted, but that I couldn't leave because it was too dangerous.

And he said they could help me with my gift.

That's what he calls it, which I think is kind of funny, but I think I sort-of get it. Or maybe he's just trying to make me feel better, but that's a nice thing to do, wouldn't you say? I think so.

So I get to live here, and every now and then they take me into the dentist's room, and they give me something so that I can't feel any pain, and then they take one of my teeth, and they put something on my eyes so I can't blink and they show me a photo, and I feel the thing in my mind and then they carefully patch me up and let me go. Honestly it's fine, look! False teeth! See, they take care of me.

I've only got a couple of baby teeth left, but they are going to keep me here and see if it works on my grown-up teeth too. Which is fine, I know how to wear dentures now anyway, and they tell me I am helping them get rid of bad people, and it's good to help, don't you think?

Well, anyway, so that's me. I hope you feel well enough to write things down soon.

I'm dying to know why they took your tongue.

The Hand

The rent is on the table, but that's okay. Because since I put it on the table, it's made friends with the next five months' rent – plucked out of the stacks of the other players and lined it up in front of me in neat multi-coloured piles. After a run of shitty luck that has all but defied belief; after heartbreak after heartbreak and loss after loss after motherfucking loss, the tide has fucking turned. I'm sweaty, stinky, and practically part of the chair – the fake-leather cushion moulded round my arse, sweat sticking my trousers to it through my pants, which are practically jammed up my crack. My balls are taking a Turkish bath but they don't itch. Not if I don't move, and I don't.

The throat of my shirt has been open for the last five hours, and the gallon and a half of Coke

I've drunk means I can actually feel the hard pulse beating. I feel flushed, and I'm sure I look drunk. Fine by me; I'm in good company. Since I sat down at the £5/£10 'big game' table at 8 p.m. I've been faced by a parade of pissheads, losers, chancers, and drifters, all apparently with money to burn and possessing not even the most basic understanding of pot-odds, and *sweet Jesus* I love London town on a Friday night.

Not that it's been particularly kind to me since I 'turned pro' (sounds a lot better than 'got laid off and decided to gamble up my redundancy payoff', doesn't it? Yeah, I think so too). In fact, the poker gods have been pissing all over me, and the only part of me not stinking of urine would be my burning teeth – if you get me.

It's been a heart-breaking, heartburning, hair pulling bitch of a month, and by the time I sat down tonight I was way beyond last-chance saloon territory. The fucking rent was on the table, and really, there was the taste of blood in my throat and just a feeling of fuck you, things can't keep going like this. Stupid thinking. Loser thinking. My heart was pounding in my chest, and all I could think was to try and play snug as fuck, hit a couple of uncontested pots, build a little stack, quit with a win. Don't think about doubling up, or being all-in; just score a profit.

But it's fucking Friday night, so what are the chances? None whatsoever. I soon realise that there's a maniac three seats to my left, playing half his hands, raising loose early, limp calling, and because everyone else is clued into him, he's getting passengers every time, building nice big family pots and firing away at flops like his chips are on fire. Fucker's up too; 2K buy-in max and he must have the best part of three and a half grand in front of him.

Fucker.

Course, the way he's winning means one of a couple of things – he's streaking, or he's up against scared money. Or a bit of both. I'm leaning to scared money. That's great news if I can shake him off and build a stack – I could run the table and make my nut easy – but that wasn't the plan, and anyway, if he's streaking that won't matter a gnat's fart in a hurricane, and I've only seen fifteen hands so that's no kind of sample size, but here I am just the same with pocket Queens in the cut-off, and he opens for fifty quid, and there's two callers to me. *God-fucking-dammit.*

I actually think about folding. Seriously. I count off the two-fifty in chips. Look at the pile. Look at the five-fifty that leaves behind. If I make this bet and then have to fold the flop, I'm fucked. I can't make the rent, even if I leave straight afterwards.

On the other hand, that fucker's playing every other hand, and the others are all just trying to catch a flop. And I'll have position on him for the whole hand.

Jacks I think I would have mucked (bad beat stories are the most boring imaginable, so let me just stay I have three fish-hook horror stories from the last month that I won't forget if I live to be a hundred) but it's Queens, and if I can just take this arsehole down, the table is *mine*.

My luck has to change sometime. It just *has* to.

Besides, he might fold.

...

'Raise.'

I move the chips across the betting line slowly, deliberately. The blinds fold fast, but Mr Maniac doesn't even look up from under his cap to call.

Of fucking course.

The others fold. Dealer taps the table, mumbles 'heads up', and here comes the flop:

10 of Diamonds. 9 of Clubs. 2 of Spades.

He still doesn't look up as he checks.

And here we are. Just over five hundred in the pot, five-fifty in front of me, fifteen hands in, and I have exactly one move open to me. He took one glance at the flop, with affected indifference, and now he's just looking down at his hands folded over his cards. Not a lot there.

Shit, shit, shit.

Here's the problem. He tends to bet flops, this guy. Not one-hundred percent, but he's seen eight flops since I sat down, and he's bet five of them. No showdowns, so fuck really knows, right? But unless he's streaking like Jesus, I know he can bluff a flop.

He's not bluffing this one.

So, either he's scared of the new player, and it's a check fold...

Or he's trapping.

Back to the board. 2/9/10, rainbow. He's not going to be check calling with two overs and a flush draw, give me ulcers to the river, at least. Good. What does that leave? 7/8 for the open-ended straight draw? Jack/10 suited, beloved of all idiots who read Super/System once without really understanding it? Is he dumb enough to think he can trap here with top pair, shit kicker?

I look at him, at his stack, and glance round at the other players. Yes, he's that dumb.

Unfortunately, that hardly exhausts the possibilities. I could already be as good as dead – to 10/10, 9/9, 2/2 and, perhaps the worst possibility, some 10/9 draw that hit top two. Possible? Hell, *likely* given my luck to this day, practically a mortal fucking lock. At least I'm not worried about Aces, Kings, Ace/King – I know I'd have heard about it pre-flop - he's exactly the kind of turdmonkey that thinks people are too stupid to notice he raises a lot with crap but three-bets only with the goods.

So cut the over pair, we've got either fuck all that folds, 10/Jack to 10/Ace that calls (and I sweat 2 cards), or two pair or the set, and I lose everything.

I don't have the time, inclination, or skill to calculate which of those is more likely statistically, but at least I know what I'm up against. Trivially obvious too that a check is as good as a fold. He moves on me regardless with the next card, and unless it's a Queen, I probably can't call.

I'd like to say that my thoughts were something macho like '*no guts, no glory*' but unfortunately, all I had left was '*fuck it.*'

'All in.'

Five hundred and fifty pounds in chips cross the line, and my hands shake not at all. My gut gurgles, my palms sweat, my heart fucking hammers in my ears like I'm going to have a fucking stroke, but I don't blush and my hands don't shake.

He looks up briefly, eyes not looking at me but the stack. Counting. I just start to exhale when he says:

'Call.'

I sit bolt upright, and the air leaves my lungs in a rush. Fuck. Fuck! I feel the room begin to draw away from me, my lips and face feel numb, like I'm retreating from the scene, having an out of body experience, and the dealer says

'Showdown. On their backs.'

From some impossible distance, and moving under their own power, my hands casually turn over my two ladies, face up on the green felt, and my opponent flips his hand, and there's not a gasp, but there is some kind of surprised reaction from the guy next to me, which I register as if from a faint radio broadcast on the edge of static, because the message coming back from my retina to my disbelieving brain is that my opponent has tabled pocket 8's.

I blink rapidly, expecting them to turn into 9's, the only thing that would make sense given my run, but they stubbornly stay 8's – lovely, lovely snowmen – and I notice a couple of grins on my right, like maybe some people have been waiting a while for this shoe to drop and they're glad, relieved even, to be at the felt when it happens. The dealer is quick enough that I barely have time for the pure elation of the moment to be diluted with anxiety about being out-drawn before he peels off a beautiful 4 of Spades on the turn and an irrelevant 7 of Hearts on the river, then indicates to me to take my winnings.

I rake the pot, tipping the dealer a £10 chip, and the world begins to wash back into focus. Next to me, a man remarks across the table to an acquaintance or friend, 'Because of course the raiser ALWAYS has Ace/King there, and just HAS to be bluffing the flop,' and his friend chuckles, and holy fuck if I don't chuckle too.

Holy mother of fucking God. I'm in the game.

My hands do shake, a little, as I stack my chips back up. Doubled up. Doubled up. Well okay, if I leave now, I've got two months' rent – or one month's rent and a roll to play the £1/£1 game again. Seat fee already came out of my pocket, so it's all profit.

I turn to the guy next to me. 'Things that you promise yourself you won't do when you sit down...' Sideways smile. Suddenly easy to smile, now.

'Don't work like that, do it? Gotta play the cards, man. Nice hand.' He smiles back; the relaxed, easy smile of the casual gambler, of a man that's never had his rent riding on the turn of a card, but that's cool, I'm grateful for the show of friendship, and all of a sudden I'm relaxed and ready to play some poker.

Which is handy, because suddenly the hands are flying thick and fast, like the poker gods turned on the good-card spigot.

Two circuits later, turdmonkey – angry and dispirited – tries a cute minimum re-raise pre-flop, and I snap-fold my steal bluff. He shows the Aces, pissed, and the very next hand he calls my button raise (three limpers, so I make it a hundred to go with cowboys) from the blinds. Everyone else folds out and the flop comes 2/8/4, Diamonds and Spades. I have no flush draw, so bet out one-seven-five into the two-fifty pot. He calls, turn's the 8 of Spades, two flush draws now – check, check, river the third 8. He bets two-fifty. I think about it, but not for long. Shove, call, King/King beats 10/10, and I've doubled up twice through the same guy, and now have the best part of three grand in front of me.

It's a blur, now – the cards, the hands, the opponents. Turdmonkey leaves, so do a couple of regulars; my opposition gets younger, drunker, more aggressive. I seem to float serenely above it all – knowing when to bluff, when to value bet, when to trap check – it seems like whatever I did last time, the cards give me the opposite, most deceitful hand next time. My stack is big enough that I'm protected now against all-comers, their 2K max buy-in can damage but not kill me, and pretty soon, as the chips pile up, they can't even really do that. I fly clean through the 4K barrier with an incredible three-barrel bluff against someone who just will not put two grand in with top pair against someone running like God, and I hit six thou with a flopped house – pocket 9's on a 9/King/King flop. Against Ace/King.

Heaven.

Dragging that pot, I become aware for the first time of an ache behind my eyes. The amount of Coke I've necked means that I'm unlikely to feel tired for several days, but I'm definitely starting to hit that uncomfortably sweaty, stretched feeling that caffeine plus sugar, plus adrenaline, plus physical inactivity creates. The table is thinning out too, finally; the two players I just felted are not replaced by fresh blood. We're down to six, and two of them (a super-tight Asian gentleman and a tired, bored-looking black man) are both yawning with an ostentation that strongly indicates the game doesn't have long left to run. Probably they'd have left already if not for the siren call of my out-sized stack, and the feeling that sooner or later, my streak has to break.

Not happening fellas, I think, but I'm happy for them to keep firing. Tonight, I'm fucking Superman. Bulletproof.

That's the moment that a hand slaps me on the back, hard, and I jolt in my chair, heart suddenly hammering very uncomfortably. My hands spasm, and I knock half my stack all over the felt. I hear a burst of wheezy laughter that I'd recognise anywhere, carried over my shoulder on a heavy breeze of fetid, whisky-soaked breath.

Fucking Nate.

Fuck it.

'You doin' all right man? Hey, fuck me, y'are! Yer fuckin killin' it, man! Fair fuckin play, look at you man; fuckin killin' it! Fuck!'

It's possible he's not entirely sober.

'Hey, Nate.'

'Hey yourself! Didn't tell me you was out tonight, ya fucker! Keepin' all the fish to yerself, yeah? Jammy cunt!'

He doesn't mean to be offensive. I'm almost certain of it.

'Yeah, look—'

'Yeah, what's that you got man, five fuckin grand? Didn't even know you played this high man, thought you were strictly one and one!' Another burst of laughter – I actually feel a fine spray of his saliva splash my cheek. My stomach does a slow flip.

Please God, don't let this perfect poker evening end with me puking on my chips.

'Nate! Yeah, man, just decided to take a shot, you know? Felt lucky.'

Self-depreciating. Apologetic. Please-go-away-and-leave-me-alone.

More of that fucking laugh, practically roaring in my ear now. Jesus, he whiffs so bad I can smell him over my own stink. If he doesn't move soon, get his sweaty hand off my back, I think I really am going to throw up.

'Fucking lucky? No shit man, you fucking cleaned up! Lucky I came along; you almost had it your own way all fucking night!'

What? Oh, fuck me, no, no, no, no...

'Hit that fucking accumulator yesterday. Been on the piss ever since.'

Voice travelling to my left, he's moving towards the empty chair.

No no no no no...

'Fuck it, easy come, easy go, right? Let's play some fucking cards.'

An obscene wedge of bills hits the felt as he sits down. I stare at it, stupidly, temporarily unable to process what is happening.

'Naw, Nate, look—'

'Don't worry, man, don't sweat! Like I said, it's whatchacallit. Found money! Ain't gonna miss it!'

Yeah, because *that's* what I'm worried about, Fuckstick.

'Honest, Nate, I was going to leave soon, I'm fucking knackered...'

This time the spit spray from the laugh goes all over his money (and I see a flicker of disgust cross the face of the dealer, too quick for Nate to notice) and the clip on my shoulder is enough to almost knock me off my chair, and as I flail and grab the edge of the table the other half of my stack spills over.

Motherfucker.

'Gonna fucking leave! Fucking good one, mate!'

He turns to mister super-tight, who has been observing this exchange with polite disbelief.

'This fucking degenerate's gonna leave while I'm putting the big cheddar down! Fucking comedi*enne*, right? Good one, man.'

I see the clip coming this time. Brace. It helps a bit.

'Naw, man, come on. Let's play some fucking POKER!'

The dealer has counted out the cash on the table quickly, and in the polite, measured tone of one experienced in delivering bad news to the intoxicated, says 'Sorry, sir, but I'm afraid you've exceeded the table limit. You've got four thousand, five hundred and eighty pounds here. Maximum buy-in is two thousand.'

Thank you, sweet Jesus. Of course he can't put down enough to stack me. Okay, fine, play with the pisshead for a little bit, let him run the table and his mouth, and beg off once he wins a couple of pots. Better yet, let one of the others stack him. Play super-snug and get the fuck home with your stack and honour intact, for tomorrow is another day. No need to take him on, no need to engage.

'Unless, of course, no one objects to raising the table limit?'

Oh no, you fucking <u>didn't</u>.

But of course, he did. And of course, mister super-tight (who's already dreaming about stacking this guy pre-flop with Aces, clearly with no fucking idea what he's up against) is eagerly indicating his supreme lack of a problem with this notion, and so it goes around the table, eager happy nods, *please let the nice drunk man sit down with his huge amounts of gambling money at stakes way above his normal limit, that would be quite fine, I'm suddenly not tired at all,* and by the time the dealer's gaze turns to me (did I see a flicker of sympathy there? Probably not) the mood of the table is very clear.

Oh fuck this.

I nearly say no anyway, 'cause just fuck this noise; I nearly just get up and leave, rack my chips and go, but they're all looking at me, with various degrees of 'do-not-tap-the-glass' in their eyes, and *fuck, fuck, fuck it,* I'm just fucked.

Exhale.

'No problem.'

Smiles all round. Nate nodding like it's a formality. A better man might feel some sympathy for what these poor saps have just unleashed on themselves. Not me. Rage, bile, and hatred clog up my throat like a physical thing. I'm choking on it, and I just want to kill every last retarded one of them, and then myself, because Nate just sat down with the best part of a five grand stack, so let the poker holocaust commence.

Not me, you fuck (I vow, again.) *Not me, not this time.*

'Let's play some fucking CARDS!'

Big grin. Red faced, barely able to focus, practically swaying in his chair. It's no act either

– I've been in the hell of this man's orbit long enough to know that. He does know a bit about poker, he's not a moron, but he's insanely aggressive and painfully lucky and I've seen him go broke many, many times...but he always fucking kills me. Every time. My fucking kryptonite.

I sweep my cards into my fist, miserably, all the good feelings of the night evaporating, the rush and the poker gods abandoning me – I actually feel them leave – and I try to mentally hunker down, calm my jangling nerves. Try really hard to just play some smart poker and get out with my stack intact.

Six month's rent and change. Get it home. Somehow, get it home. Just avoid this prick.

But it's impossible. He raises every hand. No shit. A hundred to go.

Blind.

Every hand.

The other players start to look nervous as well as excited, like they realise they're in what we like to call a high-variance situation. Lots of folds, lots of respect. That lasts for two circuits, twelve miserable hands where it's raise, fold, fold, fold, fold, take your money, and finally Mr super-tight wakes up in position with something good and calls the raise. We all know the score and get the fuck out of the way.

Flop 10/8/4 rainbow. Nate belches, then slurs 'Bet,' and throws three hundred into the pot. Super-tight snap-shoves, overexcited, already counting his money. Nate deliberates, hope warring with reason, which ends exactly how you'd predict:

'Call.'

The cards hit the felt. Super-tight caught cowboys. Nate tables 7/3. Off. Super-tight does not smile. It's like he knows. I sure as fuck do.

Turn is a Jack. The river brings the 9.

Runner/runner straight for the win.

Super-tight stands up so fast, his chair almost falls over. He's done for the night. He thrusts his hand out in congratulations, smile sick and pained. 'Nice hand, sir.'

Nate barely touches the outstretched hand. 'Thanks.' Serves him fucking right, I think.

Then I realise, with a sinking feeling in my bowels that, with the additional chips, Nate now has me covered.

One hand could cost me everything.

The rage comes back then, helpless,

powerful, but there's a new component to it – the desire for vengeance. This man has tormented me mercilessly, been the bane of my fucking life the last month, a living, breathing totem of bad fucking luck, and all of a sudden, I've had enough, and I'm glad we're playing for keeps.

Because tonight, it's going to be different. Tonight, I'm going to fuck him up for good. Found money, Nate? Fine. Finders fucking keepers.

'Nice hand, Nate.'

He smiles. 'Yeah, I just felt it was coming, you know?'

'I do indeed, Nate. I do indeed.'

I manage a smile. It even feels genuine, in its way.

We're back down to six, but the other players very quickly become non-entities, recognising somehow the battle that is about to commence.

Next hand, he comes out with the standard hundred raise, I make it a thousand. Blind. He looks up at me then, regarding me with an attempt at care, and I remember with a nasty jolt that this man is not quite as stupid as he looks. If only because that wouldn't be medically possible.

'Caught a hand, did you mate?' He hates to fold pre-flop. It's practically against his religion. But he does, and I flip over my hand indifferently as I reach for the pot. Turns out I had Jack/3 off-suit – I was hoping for 7/2, but it's enough to send a message. The others, who have watched me build this stack over several hours with great care, are agog. Let 'em be. I'm only playing one guy now.

There's a thunderstruck pause, followed by an explosion of laughter so violent that the dealer flinches. I look over, and yes, Nate has flushed an alarming brick red, the vein in his forehead is throbbing, and he's pounding the table hard enough to make his chips dance and tumble.

Eventually he manages to catch enough breath to say 'Came to play, did you? Came to fucking play! Like it man, like it. Beautiful.'

He seems genuinely pleased. I'm feeling pretty happy myself. Next hand, and he's first to act against my big blind.

'All in blind!' Happy with himself. Ecstatic, even. Flushed, sweating freely, stinking. I've seen him like this before, and I know for sure he won't stop 'till he goes broke, or the rest of us do.

Fine by me – tonight, it's gonna be fucking him. The others all check their hands, and fold disappointedly, and it comes down to me.

'Come on, call blind man! G'wan man, you know you want to!'

'Can't, man,' I say with a regretful smile, and peek at my hand.

King of Clubs, Queen of Hearts.

Interesting.

I put a chip on top of my cards to keep them safe, and look over at my opponent.

This is it. It has to be, right? I mean, he's blind, so any hand significantly above average, I just have to call, right? Fucking crazy, but that's poker, right? That's what this whole evening has been about, yeah? The poker gods putting me in this spot, to finally end the torment, once and for all.

'Fuck me, he's actually thinking about it! Hahahahaha! I fucking love you mate, I really do!'

And yeah, what the fuck am I thinking about? I've got six thousand pounds in front of me, from a lowly seven-fifty start, and if ever there was a time to give up, get up, and go home, this must surely be it.

But...

But, I have him beat, statistically. Crushed, even. Statistically, this is the right call, an easy call. Be offered this bet a thousand times, take it every time, and never have to work again. Right? This is poker; it's the nature of the game, how good players make money off bad ones. Knowing the odds and playing them.

This is the game.

Six fucking grand.

There's a sickening inevitability about it, isn't there? It feels like there is.

Fuck it, if I go broke, I'm just gonna quit, use the next two weeks to get a job, burn all the books and never look back.

It's a relief, this thought – the pressure seems to evaporate. Make the right decision, to go with all the unrewarded correct decisions I've made this month, and let the poker gods decide. Fuck it. Last time pays for all.

My heart is perfectly calm, my hands steady. I come out of my own internal processes enough to realise the room is silent, everyone is staring at me – even fucking Nate has shut up, and is looking – dear God, is he looking nervous? Could it possibly be he's suddenly woken up to the stupidity of this situation? Might it not just be that under the drunken bravado, a game was being played, and now there's a fear we're off script? I fucking hope so. I do. I smile into his ruddy, sweaty, fat face.

Last time pays for all.

'Call.'

The Garden

It's so beautiful, this time of year. The sunlight just glistens through the browning leaves of the trees, playing dappled light across the lawn. I sit on the bench, well wrapped up in my thick coat and scarf, gloved hands gripping the handle of my walking stick. The breeze is cold enough to sting my cheeks, but my glasses help protect my eyes from watering, so I can clearly watch as the leaves dance, fluttering along the grass.

So beautiful. I close my eyes, just for a moment, and allow my mind to empty; take the blessing of the light without thought, without art, for its own sake. The ground still smells damp from last night's rainfall and, as I fill my lungs deep, I can almost taste the grass pushing out of the earth, enjoying a late-year surge before the first frost stunts progress for good.

And I also scent jasmine. Unlikely, but unmistakable. It can mean only one thing and, sure enough, when I open my eyes, Jen is standing there, across the path, looking over at me. The yellowing afternoon sun is behind her, making her silhouette glow, and the brightness makes my eyes narrow, squint, and fill with water. She becomes a blurred shape, almost a shadow, indistinct, but undeniably her. And she's smiling at me, beautifully, wonderfully. She has a smile that lights her whole face, lights a whole room. Out here, with the sun behind her, it's almost too much.

"Hey, love." My own voice sounds frail, reedy, cracked. Weak. Still, I can feel my own smile on my lips, pained but real. It's good to feel. It's been a while.

"Sweetheart." She crosses the path and stops just shy of standing over me, the sun behind her now giving her a halo. She is so beautiful, almost painful to look at. Her long dark fringe plays across her face in the wind, but her blazing blue eyes don't falter as she holds my gaze. "We are well met, are we not?"

"Aye, my love. Well met we are and ever were, sure." The words begin to stick in my throat, as it constricts, and I feel my nose start to block. Eyes itching now, the tears no longer just from bright light.

Her smile widens and a single, joyous laugh bubbles from her, giving me a warm glow of pleasure right down to my boots. I'd face down the devil himself, I think then, and all the armies of hell too, if I could just carry that laugh with me when I went.

"Soft, my love, soft." She is kind, as ever – so kind, so fair. "Well met you say, and I say so too. I have loved you true, and been well loved in return."

It is too much. I sob. The tears cause my vision to refract and her form breaks, becomes fractured.

"It's not fair!" The refrain of youth from the throat of an old man. The note in my voice is desperate and plaintive, the cry of a hungry baby.

"No love, not fair, not right. But it is and it's done."

I continue to weep, great wracking sobs shaking my skeleton, burning my throat. My eyes are squeezed shut, but still I feel her near, smell her near, sense it. She is close enough to touch now, to kiss, but I can't open my eyes, can't stop bawling like a child.

"Goodbye. Remember me, and live well in my memory." Her breath in my ear is gentler than the wind, and warmer. Her scent fills my nostrils, and my lips tingle with the ghost of her kiss. Then those things pass, and she is gone. I open my eyes, too late, and there is only the lawn, and the trees, and the sky and the sun and my tears on my cheeks and the pain in my chest, my lungs labouring and my throat aching, and my eyes streaming.

Eventually, after endless minutes, my sobbing begins to taper off. I dig into my deep jacket pockets and pull out my phone. I hold it in my hand, waiting for it to ring.

Someone is going to want to speak to me soon, I am confident. Soon, the phone will ring and a voice, heavy with sympathy, will give me the dreadful news.

Any minute now.

The cold breeze has died down and I turn my face back to the sun, feel it drying the tears on my cheeks, the salt stretching the skin beneath.

I can wait.

Also by Kit Power:

Collections

A Warning About Your Future Enslavement That You Will Dismiss As A Collection Of Short Fiction And Essays By Kit Power (2017)

Novellas

The Finite (Black Shuck Books, 2019)

Non-Fiction

Tommy (Electric Dreamhouse, 2019)

blackshuckbooks.co.uk/shadows

www.ingramcontent.com/pod-product-compliance
Lightning Source LLC
Chambersburg PA
CBHW070503170726
48291CB00008B/2637